Nikalas Catlow, David Sinden & Matthew Morgan

the Funny Fingers

are going on HOLIDAY!

EGMONT

The Funny Fingers were an unusual family but
a very happy one. They loved to have fun.

"Pack your bags, everyone," said Dad, one morning. "We're going on holiday to Funworld!"

"Wahey!" cheered Finn and Flo. Funworld was brilliant – it had a Pirate Pool, Spaghetti Slides and a Fabulous Fancy Dress Parade.

Before you could say *fastest finger first*, the family were boarding their aeroplane.

"Yippee!"

"Woo-hoo!"

But the Funny Fingers weren't the only ones going on holiday . . .

Their miserable neighbours, the Terrible Toes, were taking a break too. But they hated fun so they were off to Grumpland.

"Errol, you oaf, get a move on!" Mr Toe ordered their pet foot monster.

The Funny Fingers' aeroplane whooshed up into the sky.

"Next stop: Funworld!" Finn called.

"At last, we're free of those annoying Fingers," sneered Mrs Toe.

All day long the Terrible Toes shouted at Errol. "Go left! Go right! Faster, you foolish foot!"

But it was a very long way to Grumpland, and that night, while the Terrible Toes slept in the caravan, Errol accidentally took a wrong turn.

The next morning the Terrible Toes
woke up to a BIG surprise!

"Aaaargh!" Mrs Toe screamed.
"Errol's brought us to Funworld!"

"Oh, no! Funworld's where the Funny Fingers are," moaned Mr Toe. "Get us out of here, Errol!"

But the foot monster was nowhere to be seen, because he'd gone exploring . . .

At the Funworld beach, the Funny Fingers were very surprised to see Errol hopping across the sand.

"Hey, Errol's here!" said Mum.

"Come and join the fun, Errol," called Flo.

The Funny Fingers and Errol had fun chilling out at the Incredible Edible Ice-cream Shack.

Then they had fun dressing up at Fabulous Fred's Costume Corner.

"There's a prize for the best costume at the parade later," Fabulous Fred told them.

And after such a busy morning, they went for a dip in the Pirate Pool.

"Look, Mr and Mrs Toe have come to join in the fun too," said Dad.

But Mr and Mrs Toe did not want to join in the fun.

"Oi, Errol, we're leaving!" Mr Toe shouted. "Get down from there!"

The foot monster did as he was told . . .

Splash!

"Wooooaaah!"

A huge wave swept
the Terrible Toes
from the pool . . .

. . . all the way to the Wacky Race Track!

"What a great idea, Mr and Mrs Toe, let's have a race!" Mum called.

Finn, Flo and Errol jumped into a racing car and zoomed off.

The Terrible Toes sped after them.

"Stop, Errol!"
Mr Toe ordered.

Errol did as he was told and skidded
to a halt. But the Terrible Toes
were going too fast, and shot
off the top of a sand dune . . .

"Aaaargh!"

The Terrible Toes tumbled off the bottom of the slide, and Errol landed on top of them.

"Errol, you bumbling bunion, get back to the caravan NOW!" Mr Toe shouted. "We're going!"

The Terrible Toes rushed
back to their caravan.

"Giddy up, Errol!" Mr Toe ordered.

But just as they were about to leave, the Funny Fingers came marching past in the Funworld Fancy Dress Parade.

"I've brought your costume, Errol," said Grandma.

"You don't want to miss out on the fun," said Fabulous Fred.

The foot monster certainly didn't want to miss out on the fun, so he joined the parade! But he'd forgotten he was still attached to the Toes' caravan . . .

"No, Errol, you're pulling us the wrong way!" Mrs Toe shouted.

The parade weaved past the Spaghetti Slides . . .

across the Wacky Race Track . . .

around the Pirate Pool . . .

"Waaaah!" the Terrible Toes yelled, as their caravan span round and round, faster and faster, until . . .

SNAP!

. . . the rope broke!

The caravan flew through the air and landed in the Incredible Edible Ice-cream Shack.

SPLAT!

The Terrible Toes emerged from the shack covered in ice-cream.

"Wow, great fancy dress costumes!" Dad said.

Fabulous Fred stopped the parade. "The prize for best costumes goes to the Terrible Toes!" he announced. "They win a week's holiday at Funworld!"

"NOOO!" Mrs Toe cried. "NO MORE FUNWORLD!"

"We want to go home!" Mr Toe shouted.

But with their caravan ruined, the Terrible Toes would have to wait for a lift home in the Funny Fingers' aeroplane . . .

. . . after a WHOLE WEEK of holiday fun together!

Ha ha, hee hee, ho ho!

SUN
LOTION